Foolish Goose

Written by
Shirley Simon

Illustrated by
Mary Carter

Foolish Goose went for a walk.

"Who?" called Owl.
"I am Foolish Goose,"
said Foolish Goose.

Foolish Goose came to a river.
In the river, she saw
Foolish Goose.

"Oh!" cried Foolish Goose.
"I am in the river."

Away ran Foolish Goose.

"Help!" shouted Foolish Goose.
"I am in the river."

"You are foolish, Foolish Goose. You are right here. So you cannot be in the river."

15

"Come and you will see,"
said Foolish Goose.

"See," said Foolish Goose.
"I am in the river."

Owl said, "You foolish bird. You see me in the river, too."

"But we are not really in the river. We are right here."

"Oh," said Foolish Goose.

"It is day," said Owl.
"It is time for me to sleep."

"Now who is a foolish bird?"
asked Foolish Goose.

29

"Good night, Owl,
or is it good day?"